Mail Order E
The Sheriff's S
Christmas Bride

By
Faith Johnson

```
Clean and Wholesome Western
      Historical Romance
```

Copyright © 2022 by Faith Johnson

All rights reserved.
No part of this book may be reproduced, stored in a retrieval system, or transmitted in any form, or by any means, electronic, mechanical, photocopying, recording or otherwise, without prior permission of the author or publisher.

Printed in the United States of America

Table of Contents

Unsolicited Testimonials.............. 4
FREE GIFT............................ 5
Chapter 1............................ 6
Chapter 2............................ 22
Chapter 3............................ 35
Chapter 4............................ 52
Chapter 5............................ 67
Chapter 6............................ 76
Chapter 7............................ 98
Epilogue............................. 108
FREE GIFT............................ 115
Please Check out My Other Works...... 116
Thank You............................ 117

Unsolicited Testimonials

By **Glaidene Ramsey**
⭐⭐⭐⭐⭐ I so enjoy reading Faith Johnson's stories. This Bride and groom met as she arrived in town. They were married and then the story begins.!!!! Enjoy

By **Voracious Reader**
⭐⭐⭐⭐⭐ "Great story of love and of faith. The hardships we may have to go through and how with faith, and God's help we can get through them" -

By **Glaidene's reads**
⭐⭐⭐⭐⭐ "Faith Johnson is a five star writer. I have read a majority of her books. I enjoyed the story and hope you will too!!!!!"

By **Kirk Statler**
⭐⭐⭐⭐⭐ I liked the book. A different twist because she wasn't in contract with anyone when she went. She went. God provided for her needs. God blessed her above and beyond.

By **Amazon Customer**
⭐⭐⭐⭐⭐ Great clean and easy reading, a lot of fun for you to know ignores words this is crazy so I'll not reviewing again. Let me tell it and go

By **Kindle Customer**
⭐⭐⭐⭐⭐ Wonderful story. You have such a way of showing people that opposite do attack. Both in words and action. I am glad that I found your books.

FREE GIFT

Just to say thanks for checking our works we like to gift you

Our Exclusive Never Before Released Books

100% FREE!

Please GO TO

`http://cleanromancepublishing.com/gift`

And get your FREE gift

Thanks for being such a wonderful client.

Chapter 1

Annie Robinson stepped through the front door with a basket of groceries hanging over one arm. She felt ill. The effect that her own home had on her was strange. She knew that it wasn't normal to be so nervous. She shouldn't have been shaking at the sight of her house.

However, that was her life.

From time to time, Annie would get a couple of hours to herself on the outside. Though, sooner or later, she'd always have to make it back home.

She hated coming back. She knew what it meant.

Annie held her breath as she shut the door behind her quietly. So far, she couldn't hear anything, but that could have been a bad thing.

If there was no sound of her father's snoring, it only meant that he was awake.

He was always drunk when he was awake. Annie had learned that she preferred it when he was sleeping.

She was lonely. She liked her own company even though she would have loved to have somebody to talk to. She couldn't talk to her father. He was out of the question. What would have been the point? Most of the time, he was drunk, and when he would wake, he wouldn't remember anything.

It was like looking after a child. Ever since her mother's death, Annie had felt like she had become a caregiver. She wasn't a daughter anymore. She was trapped in her own home.

Annie could smell the stench of yesterday's drunken antics in the air. She had assumed that she would have gotten used to the smell by now, but clearly, that was not the case.

After hanging up her winter coat and taking off her scarf, Annie began to walk through the house. She wondered if she could reach the kitchen without her father's snide remarks.

She realized she had been holding her breath when she walked into the kitchen. There were two empty whiskey bottles on the table. The chairs had been pushed away, indicating that her father had been active. Annie remembered pulling the chairs in before she left.

She sighed quietly before placing the basket of food on one of the counters.

Where was he?

There was no use in speculation. Annie knew that she was going to have a busy day. First, she needed to cook dinner for herself and her father. After that, there was a lot of cleaning to do.

Time always seemed to drag, but it also had a habit of slipping through Annie's fingers. Once Annie found that all of her chores were completed, the sun would have already set. It was always the same. It was as if she were a puppet. Somebody with a higher power was pulling on her strings.

She never had time for herself.

It was no life. She knew that. Yet, she couldn't bring herself to leave her father's side. He was still heartbroken after his wife's death. Perhaps his drinking was just a symptom of heartbreak. Maybe there was a good man inside of him still.

Annie had managed to put all of the food away before hearing a pair of heavy footsteps on the other side of the house.

Her heart rate picked up.

She knew what was coming.

It was inevitable, but it scared her every time.

"What took you so long?" her father came stumbling into the kitchen.

Annie pressed her lips together. It was apparent that he was drunk.

"I was getting some food," she replied quietly. "Where were you?"

Her father ignored her question. There was a deep crease between his eyebrows as he made his way past his daughter and opened up one of the cupboards. She could smell the whiskey on his breath.

Annie turned to look at him. It took him a few minutes to rummage through the cupboard beneath the window as he mumbled to himself. Eventually, he straightened up with a roll of bread in his hand and bit into it hungrily.

Anybody who didn't know him would have thought he had been starving for months.

"This bread is salty," he said while chewing. "Are you trying to poison me or something?"

Annie shook her head. "Of course not."

It didn't matter that she wasn't the one who baked it. When it came to her father, there was no logic. He would end up blaming her for everything.

"I saw that look in your eye," her father said before taking another big bite. He was swaying from side to side. "That same look... you gotta be careful, you know."

Annie nodded slowly. Most of the time, she settled for going along with his ramblings. It was the only option that seemed smart. It made no sense to challenge him.

She released a shaky breath as her eyes drifted down to the ground. She figured that she didn't need to look at him. It was better to judge his movements by sound alone.

After a few seconds of nothing but chewing, Annie saw her father's boots coming into view. He was getting closer.

"I need a drink," he said. "Where's my whiskey?"

Annie didn't know whether or not it was a rhetorical question. Her mind went blank. She didn't have the perfect reply. Anything that she would have said was bound to result in an attack. And it did.

Suddenly, she felt a sharp sting across her left cheek. The sound of a slap filled the room.

It took Annie a while to respond. Finally, she looked into her father's eyes as her own welled up with tears.

"Well?" he raised his brows. "Where is it? Did you hide it again?"

"I never hide it, father," Annie whimpered.

"You're lying to me," he growled. He smirked slightly before shoving the last bit of bread into his mouth. "You've done that before."

Annie bit down on her tongue. She was at a loss for words. There was no way that she would have ever lied to him, but that was beside the point. Nothing was ever going to be enough for him. Even if she apologized, she'd likely get another slap to the face.

By this point, it was like a routine.

"I will deal with you later," he said, shoving past her.

Annie kept her mouth closed as she listened to his footsteps stomping all over the kitchen floor. It was as if he had no particular direction. He was wandering like he was lost.

"Hiding my whiskey," he mumbled, bumping into the table. "Nobody hides anything from me. Not my daughter... it's my whiskey. She's hiding it again."

Annie gasped at a loud bang. Quickly, she turned around to see that her father was trying to walk out into the hallway but had stumbled over a chair. He shouldn't have been on his feet in the first place.

A wave of relief came over Annie when her father disappeared into another room. She heard the sound of him flopping onto the creaky mattress. She closed her eyes and began to wish for him to fall asleep.

Surely enough, after a few minutes of silence, Annie finally heard the snoring.

***

Days were starting to merge together. Often, Annie would find herself fading out of reality as her hands continued to do all of the chores. She didn't have to be present in order to get things done. The only way that she could tolerate her life was to dream of a brighter future.

Annie looked out of the window as she scrubbed a dirty plate with her tattered rag. Her hands were submerged in the warm water of the bucket. Even though she was fortunate enough to have a source of heat in her home, there was still a chill in the air.

The snow began to fall in large flakes. Annie kept her eyes on the ground to see whether or not it was going to settle.

"Annie," she heard her father's voice behind her.

Without any hesitation, she took her hands out of the bucket and turned around on her heels to face him. The water was dripping off her fingers when their gazes locked.

Something was different. He had a different look in his eye. She had never seen it before.

"Pack your things," he said, tossing a newspaper onto the kitchen table. "You're going to California."

Annie blinked. She had no idea how to reply to her father's statement.

"What are you standing around for?" he growled. "Go and pack your things!"

Despite the fear that was growing in her chest, Annie chose to stand her ground. Her curiosity was overpowering her initial urge to flee. Besides, she had the right to know why she was getting sent to a state on the other side of the map.

California was a long way away from Kentucky.

"Why am I going to California?" she asked quietly.

Surprisingly, her father decided to remain calm. He pointed to the newspaper on the table.

"I'm running out of money," he said. "I can't support both of us."

For a second, Annie thought he was kicking her out because she was just an extra mouth to feed. Her heart quivered.

"You are going over there to marry a sheriff," he continued. "He's got money. He'll be able to get us out of debt."

Annie bit down on her bottom lip. She was aware that her father wasn't particularly wealthy, but she had no idea that he was struggling to support them. It was the alcohol and the gambling. They were the two culprits of their misfortune.

She should have known that it was going to come to this eventually.

"Go and pack your things," her father reiterated. "The train is supposed to leave in a few hours."

Annie opened her mouth to speak just as her father turned around and waddled out of the kitchen. She realized that there wasn't much to say.

Obviously, she did not want to leave him on his own. He wasn't capable of taking care of himself. However, she would have been lying if she said that the idea of going to California wasn't enticing.

It was a chance for her to start a new life. It was a chance for her to live without the constant fear of getting hit. There was more to life than what she knew of it.

Annie listened to the sound of her father stumbling through the house. He wasn't drunk enough to start a fight, but it was obvious that he had had time to drink already. Perhaps Annie would be out of there before he got worse.

She glanced back at the window to look at the snow.

The idea of marrying a stranger was terrifying, but it wasn't as terrifying as the current state of her life. There was no point in debating anything. As soon as her father told her that she had to go, she knew she had no choice.

However, Annie wasn't upset.

There was hope. She had always dreamed of marrying a good man. Maybe that sheriff from California would turn out to be the man of her dreams. Furthermore, he could help her father.

He had the money, and money was important. Without it, Annie's father was bound to end up dead. He would continue drinking, and he'd lose his house.

Annie wasn't strong enough to encourage her father to seek help with his addiction. Still, maybe the money and her marriage to the sheriff were the answer to all of this.

Chapter 2

Annie took a deep breath when she finally stepped off the train.

The weather in California was warmer than it was in Kentucky, although that did not stop the thin layer of snow from forming on the ground.

Annie smiled slightly as she walked through it. She had anticipated that being so far away from her father would cause her distress, but she was wrong.

For the first time in months, Annie felt the heavy weight shifting off her shoulders. It was as if there were no burdens for her to carry. There was nothing to fear. She was a brand-new person.

She was going to meet the sheriff with whom her father had corresponded, and she would start a new life.

Annie had her future husband's name memorized.

Andrew Eastwick. Sheriff Eastwick.

He sounded like a dream.

Perhaps this was going to be the best Christmas of Annie's life.

"Annie!" a female voice called out to her. "Annie Robinson?"

Annie clenched her hand over the handle of her suitcase while she scanned her surroundings. It looked like every passerby was too busy with their own problems to notice that there was a woman running through the train platform, holding one arm up in the air.

When she got close enough to Annie, she smiled widely. "I apologize... are you Annie Robinson?"

"Yes, that is me," Annie replied. "I'm sorry... but who are you?"

The woman laughed softly, placing a hand on her chest. She had a very genuine smile.

"My name is Mary," she replied, extending her hand. "I'm Andrew's cousin. I was supposed to meet you here."

"Oh." Annie widened her eyes before shaking Mary's hand. "Pleased to meet you."

Annie assumed that Andrew would have been too busy at the office to greet her. He was a sheriff, after all. Sheriffs were always busy.

It only made everything feel more real.

"I hope that you've had a pleasant journey," Mary said, pulling away. "It must have been quite a trip coming all the way from Kentucky."

Annie nodded slowly. She realized her father must have told Andrew everything about her. She could only hope that it was the truth.

"It was a long ride," Annie replied. "But I am glad to be here."

"Well, let's not stand around any longer," Mary smiled. "It's getting cold... and you must meet Andrew. I am certain that he is stuck at his office all day. We might just catch him."

Annie quirked her eyebrow. It sounded like Mary was insinuating that Andrew wasn't aware of her arrival. Annie decided to ignore it, though. She was here now. She was here to get married.

Nothing was going to stop her.

"Please, lead the way," Annie smiled.

As both women walked through the quaint street, Annie couldn't help looking around at the buildings. All of it was different compared to her small town in Kentucky. The architecture was unfamiliar, with a lot of wood and rough brick.

Even the people were different. They all looked down as they walked. Each and every person was in a rush to get somewhere. They didn't care about anybody else's business. Not like in Kentucky.

Annie sighed in contentment as she followed Mary's lead.

The snow stopped falling just as they both reached the sheriff's office. At that moment, Annie felt her heart rate picking up. She was about to meet her future husband.

Her eyes stared at the jail sign above the office.

"I must warn you that my cousin can be quite hardheaded at times." Mary glanced over at Annie. "He spends most of his time around petty criminals and thieves. I suppose that those interactions had something to do with the way that he now talks to people."

Annie nodded in acknowledgment. "He's a sheriff. I understand."

It looked like Mary was about to say something else, but she settled for a small smile. "This way."

Annie felt her mouth drying up as she followed Mary.

Within a few seconds, both of them were inside the office. The air was warmer, though there was a distinct odor of old wood. The room was much darker than outside. It seemed like there was only one lantern providing the office with light. The small window at the front didn't do a lot to let the sun inside.

Annie closed the door behind her. The silence was louder than her beating heart.

"Mary," she heard a deep male voice. "What are you doing here?"

Annie held her breath when her eyes settled on the only man in the room. He was tall and burly. His hat was hiding most of his face from view, but she could see a hint of stubble around his jaw. Her eyes traveled lower, and she spotted a copper badge on his chest.

He was the sheriff. It was Andrew.

"I'm here to introduce you to someone," Mary replied, her voice uncertain. "This is Annie."

Andrew shifted his gaze over to Annie before nodding. "Howdy, ma'am."

"H-Hello... it's nice to meet you," Annie replied.

Her nerves took her off guard. For some reason, she felt like she wasn't prepared for this meeting at all.

Andrew placed his hands on his hips before looking back at Mary. "What is the meaning of this, Mary?"

"We talked about this before, remember?" Mary replied. "I was considering it for a long time... and in the end, I knew it was the right thing to do."

Annie was confused. When she glanced at Andrew, she could see a cloud of realization coming over his face.

What was going on?

"You didn't," Andrew said. "This isn't some kind of practical joke?"

Mary scoffed as she dropped her shoulders. "I wouldn't joke about something like that."

"But why would you do it when I told you that I didn't want to get married?"

Annie was chewing on her bottom lip. She didn't understand anything. Did she hear Andrew correctly?

"Please, let's not do this here," Mary sighed. "Can't we just have a conversation? She came all the way from Kentucky to see you."

Andrew shook his head. "The conversation should have taken place a long time ago. Unfortunately, it's too late now, Mary."

Annie felt herself tensing up when Andrew dropped his hands to his sides and approached her. He didn't allow his eyes to linger on her face. It was as if he was avoiding her gaze.

"There has been a mistake," he said. "I don't know why she told you to come here, but you should have stayed in Kentucky."

Annie widened her eyes. This was the last thing that she expected.

"I'm sorry, ma'am," Andrew added. "I have work to do."

Without any further explanation, Andrew walked past Annie and opened the door. It slammed on his way out, making her flinch.

Mary was still standing in her original spot. She looked more upset than anybody.

Annie felt her palms beginning to sweat. She bent down and placed her suitcase on the floor, then wiped her palms on her coat.

"It's okay," Mary spoke up, forcing a smile. "I will talk some sense into him."

"He didn't know about this arrangement?" Annie asked the question even though she already knew the answer.

Mary didn't respond. Evidently, she was guilty.

"You were the one who corresponded with my father, weren't you?"

Annie was aware that she was supposed to feel angry but didn't. It was as if she had been expecting disappointment. Deep down, she knew that her life was always going to remain the same. Nobody was ever going to marry her, and she'd end up living with her father forever.

"I'll talk to Andrew," Mary said, nodding to herself. "I'll talk to him and I'll make it right."

"But he will not marry me if he doesn't want to," Annie replied. "Nobody can make him."

Mary sighed as she turned to face Annie. "It's not about making him... I'm just afraid he will be sad and alone for the rest of his life. I need to... I need to talk to him. It will be alright, Annie. I promise."

Annie glanced out of the window as the feeling of melancholy surrounded her.

She didn't want to hold on to hope any longer.

Chapter 3

To save herself from further embarrassment, it only made sense for Annie to leave California behind. However, a few hours later, she was still in the state. On top of that, she had moved into Mary's house.

Andrew's cousin was overly generous. Clearly, she had a lot of love to give, but Annie couldn't help feeling guilty. The last thing she wanted was to move into a stranger's home and change the family's whole dynamic. Mary was a mother and a wife. She had more important things to take care of.

Nevertheless, Annie forced herself to stay. If she was going to leave for Kentucky, she would do it tomorrow. No trains were running for the rest of the day anyway, and she was exhausted from traveling.

Annie ran her hand over the soft duvet on top of the bed. Mary had given her a spot in the spare room of the house.

She thought about her father again. It was hard for Annie to understand how a stranger could be so kind to her when her own father wasn't.

Annie listened to the running footsteps outside of her door. Mary's two children were chasing after one another. They'd squeal in delight from time to time. It must be blissful to be so carefree and oblivious.

She wrapped her fingers around her braid as she sat on the edge of the bed. Annie wasn't particularly hungry, so she had decided to skip dinner. Mary had been too kind already. She didn't want to overstep any boundaries.

After a while, Annie glanced up at the grandfather clock by the door to see that she had been sitting in one spot for over an hour. However, just as she was about to get up, Mary walked through the door.

Annie jumped up anyway.

"I talked to Andrew," Mary said, her hands clasped together at the front. "Are you still up for it?"

For a second, Annie felt confused. "For what?"

"Getting married," Mary smiled. "We had a long conversation... and I made him see sense. He's... he said that he was willing to do it."

Annie swallowed hard. It appeared as though she had been upset over nothing.

However, she was curious how Mary had managed to change his mind so fast. When Annie met him at the office, Andrew seemed adamant that he wanted to be alone.

"The preacher is at the church," Mary added. "He will wait for you both... it will be a quick ceremony."

Annie didn't know why she was questioning the whole affair in her head. She traveled to California to get a husband. It was going to happen. So what was holding her back?

She was close to shaking her head, but when she thought about her father, it seemed like her decision had been made. Annie couldn't leave him to drink for the rest of his days. She needed to marry so that she could pull him out of that hole.

Besides, her father was the one who sent her here. It was his decision too. She had to respect that.

"Can I get a glass of water before we go?" Annie asked.

Mary's smile widened at her response. "Of course."

***

Annie had always dreamed about her perfect wedding. She used to spend a lot of time picturing herself walking down the aisle. At the end of it stood her ideal husband. In her head, the idea was always flawless.

However, as Annie glanced down at the ring on her finger, she realized that she was still walking around with a knot in her stomach. Surely, she was supposed to feel anything but that.

She was supposed to feel happy, but it felt impossible since her husband was incapable of cracking a smile.

Andrew looked like getting married was an inconvenience.

Annie stopped in her tracks when they both walked out of the church. Mary was still inside. She was probably talking to the priest.

"Are you alright?" Andrew asked, furrowing his eyebrows.

Annie looked up at him and nodded. "I just... I can't believe that I'm married."

"Me neither," Andrew replied. He seemed distant.

Annie had to wonder whether or not Mary had lied to her about Andrew's motives. She said that he was willing to get married, but it was obvious that he was miles away from the present.

The sun was close to setting, and the street in front of them was getting darker. Annie continued to fiddle with the ring on her finger as Andrew stood next to her. She was eager to find out more about him. He was her husband, after all. But Annie forced herself to stay silent. Evidently, Andrew wasn't in the best mood. She didn't want to vex him. On the contrary, she wanted to be perfect for him. A perfect bride.

"Sorry that I took so long!" Mary sighed deeply when she burst out from the church entrance. "Are you two ready to go?"

Andrew clenched his jaw as he glanced over at his cousin. "We will head home. It's getting late."

It took Annie a while to realize she wasn't coming back with Mary. She had a husband. They were going to share a home.

Suddenly, her stomach dropped. She was nervous. Was it going to be hard for her to talk to Andrew without Mary's presence? She had never had to do it before.

Annie bit down on her lip. "I need to get my suitcase."

Mary nodded slowly. "I will drop it off for you in the morning. There is no point in going back and forth now."

"Mr. Eastwick, is your house far from here?" Annie looked up at Andrew.

It seemed like he needed to concentrate in order to answer her question. "It's not far. But it's on the other side of town."

Mary nodded again. Her smile was growing at every interaction between Andrew and Annie. It was as if she had higher hopes for the marriage than Andrew did.

"You'll ride on the back of his horse," Mary said. "Don't worry... he's a good driver. He has a lot of experience with horses."

Annie took a deep breath. She was more afraid about the state of her marriage than the horse.

"I will see you tomorrow, Annie," Mary took a step forward and grabbed her hand. She squeezed it gently, casting a glance at Andrew as he approached his horse. She lowered her voice before speaking again. "Give my cousin a chance.

He is a good man, and he will be a good husband to you."

Annie couldn't help the tears that were welling up in her eyes. She looked down at the ground so that Mary wouldn't see them.

She had no doubts that Andrew was a good man. But was Annie a good woman?

He did not want her in his life, but she had stuck by anyway.

"Goodnight, Annie," Mary said, letting go of her hand.

Annie faked a smile once her tears were gone. "Goodnight, Mary."

When she turned around to look at Andrew, he was already leading his horse closer to the church. He gestured to the saddle with one hand before extending it to Annie.

"I'll help you up, ma'am," he said.

Annie took a deep breath before approaching him. "Thank you."

She squeezed his hand and noticed that his grip on her was strong. Andrew didn't seem like a man who wanted to waste any time. He grabbed her by the waist and lifted her up onto the back of the horse.

Annie felt herself floating through the air. It was like she had no control over her own body. She only noticed that the horse was trotting when the cold wind was blowing through her hair. At that point, she had to wrap her arms around Andrew's torso to stay on.

Neither one of them talked for the whole ride to his house. There wasn't much to say.

***

Annie woke up the next day in her marital bed, but Andrew wasn't by her side. She wasn't surprised to wake up alone. What else was she expecting?

She sat up slowly and looked around the room. Everything looked different when it was coated with the morning light. She could see that the sky outside her window was just starting to brighten.

Annie cleared her throat before getting out of bed. Even though her initial experience in California wasn't to be envied, she felt a lot more positive today.

She was determined to get to know Andrew. She wanted to feel closer to her new husband. They were married now. She had to make an effort. It was the least he deserved after being pushed into the whole ordeal.

Annie ran a hand through her hair as she looked down at her nightgown. Luckily, Andrew had been kind enough to provide her with the garment last night. It was a nightgown that Mary had left years ago when she stayed over at his house. The rest of her belongings were packed away, and she still had to wait for Mary to drop off her suitcase.

It took Annie a couple of minutes to pull on yesterday's clothes and walk out of the room. Once she was out, she saw Andrew by the front door. He already had his copper badge on his chest. He was putting on his hat.

"Good morning." Annie smiled slightly.

Andrew turned to her slowly. There was no sign of a smile on his face. "Good morning, ma'am."

"Are you going somewhere already?" Annie asked, playing with her fingers. She was desperate to spark a conversation, but it seemed that Andrew had other plans.

"I'm on duty," he replied. "I'll be back before sunset."

Annie raised her eyebrows. "Sunset? But... what about breakfast?"

"I'll eat at the office," Andrew said, opening the front door. "Mary should be here soon. Have a good day, ma'am."

Annie opened her mouth to speak, but the door slammed before she could say anything.

The fact that Annie had not woken up earlier brought back the feeling of guilt.

What kind of wife would send her husband off to work on an empty stomach? Was she incapable of being good to him?

Annie had the urge to wallow in self-pity, but she knew that it wouldn't have changed anything. She had to make things right. She wasn't going to be a terrible wife. She was going to be perfect for Andrew.

She sighed deeply as the cold chill from the door brushed past her arms.

Andrew's home wasn't anything special. Since he was the sheriff, it was clear that he was spending most of his time in town. That explained why the house looked like it hadn't been cleaned in a while.

Annie set her eyes on the small kitchen and began to do her duties as a wife. The more she worked, the more confident she started to feel.

Perhaps this was all that Andrew needed. He was craving this kind of companionship. He wanted somebody to take care of him, but he didn't know it yet.

Annie bit her lip in concentration when she cleaned the hardwood floors with a damp cloth. With each passing second, she felt more determined. Andrew could warm up to her. She just had to prove that she could be a good wife.

How could he know what he truly wanted if he never had a chance to experience it in the first place?

The next time Annie looked up at the clock by the front door, she realized that two hours had flown by. She straightened up and wiped some sweat off her forehead. She had been working hard for the whole morning.

Annie decided that after Mary stopped by, she'd go to town to see her husband.

She would be attentive, because that's what a good wife would have done.

Chapter 4

Annie felt like a brand-new person as she walked down the snowy street with a basket under her arm. She was aware that the feeling wasn't going to last. She was wearing a mask, and sooner or later, she'd have to take it off. Though, it was essential to wear it for now.

She was determined. She knew what she had to do.

After Mary's visit, Annie got ready as quickly as possible before making her way into town.

The street was bustling with people. Most of them carried baskets of food, just like Annie. They were probably getting ready for Christmas. It was only two weeks away.

Annie's eyes lit up when she saw the familiar sign of the sheriff's office. She made sure that her hair didn't look like a mess in the reflection of a window to her left. She was ready to see Andrew.

A part of her was excited, but she was mostly terrified.

She was hoping for a warm welcome. She didn't know him too well. He could have hated surprises.

Annie took a deep breath before exhaling the fog from her mouth. She was prepared to take a risk.

It didn't take her long to cross the distance to the sheriff's office. When she climbed up on the porch, she reached out and opened the front door without knocking. The smell of old wood was still there when she walked in.

She scanned her surroundings quickly as the door shut behind her. There was nobody in the room except for a young-looking man who was hovering by the main desk. He looked up at Annie and smiled.

"Good morning, ma'am," he greeted her. "Can I help you?"

Annie smiled back. Her gaze dropped to the badge on his chest. It was different from the one that Andrew had on his. The man must have been a deputy.

"Hello," Annie replied. "I'm looking for Sheriff Eastwick. I brought him some dinner for later."

The deputy seemed surprised as his eyes glanced towards the basket in her hands. "I apologize... but who are you?"

"I'm his wife," Annie replied.

The deputy looked very apologetic. He raised his hands in the air and nodded quickly. "Where are my manners? I haven't even introduced myself. I'm John. I'm the deputy here."

Annie smiled. "It's nice to meet you."

"I didn't realize that Andrew had a wife," John scratched the back of his head. "He never told me."

It wasn't comforting to know that Andrew might have been keeping their marriage a secret, but Annie decided not to dwell on it. She still had her hopes.

She was about to reply when she heard the distant sound of a jail cell door shutting. A few seconds later, Andrew walked out from behind the wall near the main desk. When his eyes locked with Annie's, he stopped in his tracks.

"Hi again," Annie smiled brightly.

She half expected for him to ignore her, but she was pleasantly surprised when Andrew cracked a small smile. "What are you doing here, ma'am?"

"I brought you some food," she said, taking a step towards the desk. She placed her basket on top of it and pulled back the white cloth to reveal a few bread rolls and a pot that was holding beans and rice. "I know that you didn't have a chance to get any breakfast at home, so I wanted to drop this off for you."

Andrew looked down at the basket. His deputy had to turn around to hide his smile. Annie tilted her head to the side.

"Is this alright?" she asked. "I hope that I wasn't interrupting anything."

"No, ma'am," Andrew sighed. "You didn't interrupt. Thank you for this. You... you didn't have to do this."

"I know I didn't," Annie said. "I wanted to."

A brief silence filled the room. It was possible to hear the rolling of wagons and the chattering of locals on the street.

Annie bit down on her bottom lip before stepping backward awkwardly.

"Well... enjoy your dinner," she said. "When can I expect to see you at home?"

Andrew looked like he was consumed with deep thoughts. Somehow, he always managed to look like he wasn't present. Annie began to realize that it wasn't anything personal. It was just how Andrew was.

"It won't be anytime soon, ma'am," John spoke up before walking over to the brick wall by the door and taking a yellowing paper off one of the nails. "We have a lot of planning to do before we all ride out after Max Cross."

Annie quirked an eyebrow as she turned to John. "Who is Max Cross?"

"He's an outlaw, ma'am," John explained. "We've been trying to catch him for months... and now, he's in California. We're going to gather all the deputies in town and ride out with the sheriff."

Annie felt her stomach sinking. She turned to look at Andrew and saw that he was clenching his jaw. It seemed like he didn't want his deputy to continue talking.

They were going to ride after an outlaw? Why hadn't Andrew mentioned this before?

"Isn't that dangerous?" Annie asked, glancing between the two men in front of her. "What is Max Cross wanted for?"

"He's a murderer—"

"That's enough," Andrew cut him off. "Let's change the subject."

The deputy nodded slowly before turning around to hide himself from Annie's wide eyes. It was too late. He had already said too much.

She stared up at her husband. At first, she was certain that it was a joke. There was no way that Andrew was planning on hunting down a killer.

"Is this true?" Annie asked.

Andrew had trouble lifting his eyes off the ground. He began to pace. "It's my job."

"To go after a murderer?" Annie placed a hand on her chest. "Can you not hire a bounty hunter?"

"It will be quicker this way," Andrew replied. "Don't worry about it, ma'am. I've been doing this for years."

Annie could tell that he wasn't speaking the whole truth. Clearly, this was to be something to worry about.

"I don't want you to get hurt," Annie dropped the volume of her voice. She had no right to tell Andrew how to be a sheriff. However, she had the right to be concerned. She was his wife.

Andrew reached down to his desk and shifted a few objects around before replying.

"I won't get hurt, ma'am. Like I said... this is my job. It's what I do."

Annie looked back down to the basket.

Her fate couldn't possibly be that cruel to her. She couldn't lose a husband so soon. She was just beginning to rebuild her life. It wouldn't have been fair.

Clearly, if Andrew was to die on his mission, Annie would have to move back to Kentucky. She wasn't ready to give up on her new life that easily. Selfishly, she started to wonder if things would have been different if Andrew wasn't a sheriff.

More than anything, she wished that her fate had built a clear path for her. It was never clear. There was always something that had to catch her off guard.

Though, she supposed that was exactly what life was. It was unpredictable. Sometimes, it was cruel.

Annie wrapped her arms around herself as she looked down at her boots. Was she going to have to spend Christmas alone?

"Did you get here on a horse?" Andrew asked her after a while.

Annie glanced up at him to see that he had a somber expression on his face. "No, I walked."

"Well, I can get you a wagon back to the house," Andrew said. "Allow me to walk you out, ma'am. I'm sure that you have better things to do than to spend your time around two lawmen."

Annie sighed before following Andrew to the front door. He wasn't just a lawman to her. He was her husband. Why couldn't he see that?

"Goodbye, ma'am," the deputy called out behind her. "It was a pleasure to meet you."

Annie forced herself to smile as she glanced over at Jack. "It was nice to meet you too, deputy."

As soon as she stepped outside with Andrew, she noticed that he was waving to a stagecoach driver parked on the other end of the street. It must be nice to be a sheriff. All the locals knew who he was and were ready to tend to his needs before everybody else's.

"I do appreciate the food, ma'am," Andrew said, standing beside her. "I didn't expect you to come by like that."

Annie shrugged one shoulder, keeping her arms folded over her chest as the cold wind blew past them. "I just didn't want you to be hungry for the whole day."

When she glanced over at him, she could see a small smile on his face. The snow was falling all around them. Some of the flakes were sticking to his stubble.

Annie couldn't help but admire him. Andrew was a handsome man. He must have gotten a lot of attention over the years. How did he live without a wife for so long? Was it all down to his refusal to marry?

"Here it comes," Andrew said, gesturing to the stagecoach that was turning by the office. "Michael is a friend... he will drop you off for free. Just bear in mind that he likes to sing a lot."

Annie smiled up at Andrew in amusement. "He likes to sing?"

"He's not very good at it," Andrew replied.

The stagecoach came to a standstill by the porch of the law department. Annie watched as Andrew stepped down to say something to the driver. A few seconds later, he waved over to Annie.

"It's all yours, ma'am."

Annie sighed and walked over to the door of the wagon. She thanked Andrew when he opened the door for her. Despite everything, Andrew was a true gentleman. He was a kind person and a caring husband.

Annie climbed into the stagecoach and fixed the bottom of her dress when Andrew shut the door behind her.

She bit down on her lip as the wheels began to go round. When the stagecoach got to the end of the street, Annie turned in her seat to look through the small window on the door. She noticed that Andrew was still standing on the porch. He was watching her leave.

Chapter 5

Annie had her hands on her hips as she looked down at the big bag of potatoes on the floor. It would take her quite some time to peel and roast them. First, she had to make sure everything was going to go according to plan.

Time was ticking. The holiday was only a week away, and there was still so much to do. She turned back to her notes and checked a recipe, thinking.

Suddenly, she heard the handle on the front door rattling. It swung open to reveal Andrew.

When his eyes landed on his new bride, he looked surprised.

"Oh... hello, ma'am," he said. "I assumed that you would have been asleep already."

For a second, Annie was confused. Then, she glanced out the window to see that it was completely dark.

"I didn't realize it was so late," she said.

Andrew nodded before stepping in and shutting the door behind him. He took off his coat and hung it by the door. His hat came off next.

Annie pressed her lips into a thin line when he took the badge off his chest and dropped it into a drawer of one of the cupboards. It was so easy to forget that he was the sheriff. Her husband was the sheriff.

"I've made dinner," Annie said, trying to turn her mind away from the sorts of fates that befell sheriffs. "Are you hungry?"

Andrew glanced up at the clock. Annie prepared herself for rejection, but it never came.

"Sure, ma'am," he replied. "I could eat."

Annie felt a smile coming onto her face at his answer. She made her way over to the fireplace and began to scoop the stew into a big bowl. Andrew came home late often, and sometimes she did not even see him for dinner.

When Annie turned around to place the bowl in front of him, she noticed that he was reading one of the papers. His head was tilted to the side.

"What is this?" he asked.

Annie grinned slightly as she set the bowl on the table. "It's just some stuff for Christmas... I've been planning a meal."

"A meal?" Andrew grabbed his spoon slowly. "It seems like there is enough food on there to feed a whole ranch."

Annie couldn't help giggling. She sat down opposite Andrew and pulled all the papers together. "It's for Mary and her family. I thought that it would be nice to prepare a dinner for them. She's always busy... and I finish my chores before midday."

Andrew rubbed his jawline with one hand. "You want to prepare Christmas dinner for Mary's family?"

"Well... yes," Annie replied, tucking a strand of hair behind her ear.

She was anxious that Andrew wouldn't have liked the idea, but her nerves were put at ease when he offered her a warm smile.

"I think that Mary would like that very much," Andrew said.

Annie grinned widely when he looked down at the stew bowl and finally began eating. It was the reassurance that she needed. However, she couldn't help but feel like Andrew wasn't saying everything that he wanted to say. Perhaps it had something to do with the fact that he was the sheriff. A sheriff had to be tough.

Either way, Andrew's words were enough to encourage Annie to continue with her meal plan. It was her way of thanking Mary for being so hospitable. Without Mary, Annie would have still been living in her father's little house.

The thought made a shiver go down her spine. She couldn't imagine living there again.

"Are you not going to eat, ma'am?" Andrew asked before his spoon clanked against the empty bowl. The sound brought Annie back to reality.

"Oh, I've already eaten," she replied. "I think that I'm going to stay up for a while longer. I want to make sure that I have the whole list of ingredients."

Andrew got up to his feet before scratching the back of his neck. "Can I help you with anything?"

Annie quirked an eyebrow.

"I must admit that I am not much of a cook," Andrew grinned. "But I can always help you with bringing all the food to the house. I guess that I could hire Michael and his wagon again."

It felt good to know that Andrew was so on board with Annie's plan. She had never expected him to do anything.

However, if Andrew was offering his help, Annie wasn't going to reject it.

"That would be great," she smiled. "I had trouble dragging that bag of potatoes through the snow today. I'm not going to turn down a wagon ride."

Andrew furrowed his eyebrows. "Why didn't you ask me? I'm always at the office."

"I didn't want to disturb you," Annie replied, glancing at her feet. "You're busy. I get that."

"Still, I'm your husband," he said. "I'm supposed to be supporting you, ma'am.

It doesn't matter how busy I am... I would always put you first."

Annie pressed her hand against her stomach when she felt a flock of butterflies taking flight. She had always known that Andrew was a good man, but it felt different to hear him say such words.

Nobody had ever put Annie first before. Not even her own father.

"Thank you for dinner, ma'am," Andrew sighed. "It was delicious."

Annie found her voice only when Andrew placed his empty bowl into the soapy water by the pots. "You're welcome," she said. "Have a good night."

"You too, ma'am," Andrew replied.

She got a feeling that Andrew wanted to linger instead of going to bed, though something seemed to be stopping him.

Annie understood that he might not have wanted to show his true emotions just yet. They were still freshly married.

She was capable of being patient. She was happy as long as Andrew wasn't feeling like he had been forced into a marriage that was suffocating him.

Luckily, he seemed content around her. That was all that Annie could have asked for.

Chapter 6

A week before Christmas, Annie woke up with a smile on her face. The holiday was coming up, and there was still so much to do, but none of that scared her. She was excited.

She couldn't remember the last time that she felt so overjoyed about an upcoming event.

Annie sprung out of bed and got dressed as quickly as she could. On top of the big meal for Mary's family, she also wanted to decorate the house. It wouldn't have been Christmas without some decking.

She made her way through to the kitchen to see that Andrew was already pulling on his boots. He was about to head out to work. If Annie hadn't witnessed him sleeping on the armchair a few days ago, she would have assumed that Andrew went through life without ever closing his eyes.

"Good morning," she smiled brightly as he reached for his copper badge.

Andrew looked up at his wife and gave her a curt nod. "Morning, ma'am. How did you sleep?"

"Very well, thank you," she replied. "It's still early... would you like some bacon before you leave?"

Andrew smiled slightly before getting up on his feet. He grabbed his coat off the nail and shrugged it over his shoulders. "Not today, ma'am. It's going to be a busy day at work."

"Oh, really?" Annie tilted her head in curiosity. "What is happening?"

There was a brief silence before Andrew replied. He seemed hesitant. "Max Cross."

"Max Cross?" Annie asked.

It took a few seconds for realization to spread across her face.

"The murderer?"

Andrew sighed deeply. He fixed his gun belt around his torso and buttoned up his coat. "According to our findings, he will be passing through the area today. We can't miss him. He's been wreaking havoc for months."

"I'm sure that he has," Annie stepped forward. "Do you have to be there?"

"I want to make sure that my deputies will be alright, ma'am," he replied. "I can't leave them."

"That doesn't answer my question."

Andrew glanced up at Annie. Clearly, he had not been expecting such a response from her.

He shook his head and sighed. "We've been planning this for a long time."

"I don't want you getting hurt," Annie replied. "You've not mentioned the outlaw for a while... I assumed that you weren't going to go through with this."

Andrew placed his hands on his hips as he stood by the door. He wanted to leave, but he couldn't. He was a lot like Annie. He didn't want to run away from an important conversation. It didn't feel right.

"I'll be fine, ma'am," he sighed. "I'm the sheriff."

Annie took a deep breath as she looked around the room helplessly. There had to be something that she could say to stop him.

She wasn't comfortable with sending her husband into danger like that. Sheriff or not.

"Stay in town," Annie suggested. "Please... just stay. Your deputies can catch Max Cross without your help. They are more than capable."

"Ma'am, they need me."

"I need you too," Annie said. "I need you more than they do. You're my husband."

Andrew frowned before lowering his gaze to the ground. "Like I said... I will be fine. You can expect to see me later in the evening."

"I don't want you to go," Annie reiterated. "Please, just listen to me. I have a bad feeling about this."

There was no way to convince Andrew. His cousin was right when she said that he was hardheaded. Annie could see that trait in him now.

She folded her arms across her chest when Andrew opened up the door. Some of the snow from outside floated into the room. Andrew's big frame was blocking most of it.

"Have a good day, ma'am," he said, daring to look her in the eye.

Annie couldn't find the strength to reply. Instead, she stared at him until he shut the door and disappeared from view.

***

Annie's plans for the whole day went out of the window after learning about the news of Andrew's pursuit of the outlaw. How could she force herself to do chores when her husband could be dead already?

She glanced up at the clock. Midday.

Andrew and his deputies must have already been out of town. He was out there. He was putting himself in danger.

Annie chewed on the inside of her cheek as she paced the floor. She couldn't think about anything else. Her thoughts were consumed by Andrew's actions.

She should have tried harder to stop him. She should have grabbed him and held on.

Annie pinched the bridge of her nose when she finally came to a standstill. Her heart was hammering against her chest. She was so scared.

It was foolish of her to believe that Andrew would have listened. Despite the rings on their fingers, they were practically strangers. Andrew was his own man. On top of that, he was the sheriff.

Annie took a big gulp of air as her foot tapped against the hardwood floor beneath her. Once again, all that she could do was hope. It was the only power that she had.

Annie stopped breathing when she heard the distant galloping of horse hooves. Somebody was racing past her home.

It could have been Andrew. Perhaps he had realized that he had been wrong. Maybe he was coming back.

Annie felt her mouth going dry as she ran up to the nearest window and looked out.

Her heart dropped at the sight before her.

She could see Deputy John galloping towards the house. Andrew was on the back of the deputy's horse, but it appeared he was barely managing to sit straight. His head was hanging low.

It took Annie a moment to realize that she could see a patch of red on his leg. Was it blood?

"Oh, no," she whispered.

Without hesitation, she rushed to the front door and flung it open.

"Over here!" she yelled. "Come through here!"

Annie found herself whimpering as she got closer to the verge of tears.

Deputy John worked fast. He slowed his horse and hopped off the saddle before reaching over to Andrew and pulling him down. Once his feet touched the ground, it was evident that he could not stand. The deputy had to wrap an arm around his torso to keep him upright.

"Clear the way, ma'am!" Deputy John yelled back. "I'm bringing him inside!"

Annie covered her mouth with both hands before following the deputy's orders. She shuffled backward as John brought Andrew inside. Up close, his injury looked a lot worse.

"What happened?" she asked, struggling to keep herself calm.

"A stray bullet," the deputy explained. "Ma'am, where is the nearest bed?"

Annie pointed in the direction of the bedroom with a shaky hand. "It's over there."

Deputy John nodded and darted towards the bedroom with his sheriff. Andrew groaned every time his injured leg touched the ground. At least he was still conscious.

He was still alive.

"I'm going to ride into town and find a doctor," Deputy John said after dropping Andrew onto the bed. "He needs professional help. He's bleeding."

Annie bit down on her lip as she threw herself toward her husband. She didn't know where she found the strength to lay him down properly.

There was so much blood.

"Here," the deputy said as he reached down for his belt and pulled it out of the loops of his pants. "Take this. This should help with stopping the blood flow."

"Thank you," Annie replied, grabbing it. "You will be back, yes?"

"I'll be back as soon as I can," John said before turning around and running towards the door. "Make sure that he stays awake, ma'am!"

A few seconds later, Annie heard the sound of a galloping horse. Then, the galloping faded into silence.

Annie looked down at Andrew as she perched herself on the edge of the bed. She had no time to waste. She had to be quick. This was a life-or-death situation.

She reached over to Andrew's leg and wrapped the belt around his thigh. When she pulled it tight, he groaned from the pain.

"Does that hurt?" she asked, her hands shaking as she found the closest loop.

"No, I feel fine," Andrew replied. "It's just a graze."

Annie shook her head before looking at his face. "I told you not to go. I knew that this was dangerous!"

Instead of saying anything else, Andrew shut his eyes. He knew that he was in the wrong. Perhaps it was his pride that was stopping him from having that conversation.

Annie sighed deeply. She reached for his hat and pulled it off his head. Her heart continued to race. She couldn't slow it down.

"Please, stay awake," she said. "The deputy said that the doctor will be here soon, okay?"

Andrew nodded slightly. "Yes, ma'am. I ain't tired anyway."

"You shouldn't be cracking jokes right now," Annie replied. "I thought that you were dead!"

Andrew opened his eyes to look at her. "Why would you think that, ma'am?"

"Because you were chasing an outlaw," Annie replied. "I thought that..."

She couldn't finish her sentence. Her tears finally spilled from her eyes. Annie dipped her head into her shoulder to hide from Andrew's gaze. Strangely, she did not want to cry in front of him. She didn't want him to think that she was weak.

Annie took a deep breath to regain control of her emotions. It surprised her when she felt Andrew's hand coming over hers. He began to stroke her skin with his thumb.

***

The doctor took off his spectacles and placed them in his case before closing it shut.

"Well, I packed his wound and stitched it up the best that I could," he said, standing up. "But I am putting him on bed rest for the next few weeks."

The doctor glanced over at Andrew and sighed.

"I'm sorry, sheriff," he said. "You know how it is."

Despite being shot in the leg, Andrew seemed to be in great spirits. He nodded at the doctor.

"I understand," Andrew replied. "Thank you."

Annie kept her arms around herself when the doctor grabbed his suitcase and headed towards the door. Deputy John stepped forward with a small smile.

"It's alright, ma'am," he said. "I will walk him out. I have to get going too."

"Oh, thank you, deputy," Annie said. "You will keep us updated with the news about Max Cross, yes?"

"Definitely," John said. "I'll be back tomorrow to let you know if he's been caught."

The deputy looked over Annie's shoulder to nod at Andrew.

"Get well soon, sheriff," he said. "I'll do my best at the office."

Andrew grinned slightly. "I know that you will."

Since Andrew had been shot in the leg, he figured it was best to put one of the deputies in charge until he got better. So from now on, Deputy John was going to take care of the town.

Annie felt like she had the doctor to thank. Undoubtedly, Andrew would have gone into the office the next day if he weren't on bed rest. That man didn't know when to stop. He was constantly on the move.

When the doctor and the deputy left, Annie turned back to Andrew to see that he was trying to sit up against the wall.

"Here." Annie sighed before stepping forward and fixing the pillow behind his back.

"Thank you, ma'am," Andrew cleared his throat. "I feel like I'm getting old. I can't even reach behind my back anymore."

Annie shook her head slowly as she sat herself down on the bed again. Andrew kept his eyes on her. It was obvious that she couldn't make light of the situation, but that didn't mean that Andrew would stop trying.

"I know you were worried, ma'am," he said, looking down at his leg. "But you know it's my duty."

"I understand," Annie replied. "I do. But now you have to heal. You're going to be here for weeks. Oh, my goodness... I have to tell Mary. She probably doesn't even know about what happened."

Andrew sighed softly. The morphine the doctor had injected into his leg was helping. He didn't seem to be in pain anymore.

"I was so scared," Annie said. "I wasn't prepared to say goodbye to my husband."

"You won't have to, ma'am," Andrew replied, furrowing his eyebrows. "I'm still here."

"I know, but you almost weren't," she said.

"I was thinking about you when I got shot," Andrew admitted.

Annie raised her brows at his words. It was the last thing that she was expecting to hear.

"I was thinking about how you were going to beat me with a frying pan," Andrew grinned. "That you would be so angry I got shot, you'd wish me dead."

Annie couldn't help rolling her eyes, although a small laugh escaped her lips. Andrew chuckled too.

"But mostly... I was thinking about what would have happened to you if I truly died," Andrew sighed.

Annie tilted her head to the side. "And what would have happened?"

"Well, you would have received all of the money in my will," he said. "You would have gotten to keep the house... but I was worried about your next husband. We didn't get a lot of time together... and it wouldn't have been fair."

Annie didn't know whether to laugh or cry. "You were worried that I was going to remarry?"

"Of course, ma'am," he grinned. "If I ever got to Heaven, I would have regretted not spending enough time with you."

She smiled slightly as their gazes locked. It became hard to look away. "I didn't know you felt that way about me."

"You're a wonderful person," Andrew said. "I know that I didn't show it... but I truly feel like the luckiest man on earth."

Annie felt her heart flutter. Andrew's words took her by surprise. She had been so wrapped up with worry and the upcoming plans for Christmas that she hadn't had the chance to consider his true feelings.

She had trouble hiding her smile when she felt Andrew's fingers squeezing around her hand again. He was no longer trying to hide it. He was in love with her.

Annie would have been lying if she said that she didn't feel the same way.

All that it took was a bullet for them to realize their feelings.

Annie leaned forward slowly to close the gap between them. When their lips touched, life felt like a fairytale. It was even better than what Annie had imagined before getting married.

She had her husband, but he wasn't perfect. He had his flaws. Everybody had flaws. Even Annie couldn't see herself as being the perfect bride anymore. All this time, she was striving for a fantasy. However, what she had in front of her was better.

Annie couldn't be happier.

Chapter 7

It was the night before Christmas, and Annie was quite busy. Before Andrew had gotten shot, she'd had big plans for the day. She was going to prepare a large meal for Mary's family. It was supposed to be the best day of the year.

However, as Annie looked into her empty cupboards, she realized her time was almost up. While looking after Andrew, she didn't get the chance to buy all the ingredients she needed. Instead, she had been spending most of her time inside the house, tending to Andrew. She had not wanted to leave his side.

But now, Annie sighed in disappointment. She didn't want to let anybody down.

"What are you doing, Annie?" she heard Andrew's voice behind her.

When she turned around, she saw her husband leaning against the wall. Her eyes widened as she ran up to him. "You're not supposed to be out of bed!"

"Ah, I feel fine," Andrew shrugged. "I can still get around the house."

Annie wrapped her arms around him, forcing Andrew to lean against her instead. "Would you at least take a seat? You're making me nervous. I don't want your stitches to come undone."

She could tell Andrew didn't want to appear weak, but he didn't complain. A big sigh left his lungs before he sat down on one of the kitchen chairs. He stretched his leg out in front of him.

Annie discovered that Max Cross had been caught a couple of days ago. There was another shootout. Luckily, nobody else from the law department got injured.

"I thought that you've already made dinner," Andrew said.

"I did," Annie smiled slightly. "I was just thinking about tomorrow."

"We have food for tomorrow," Andrew replied, glancing around the kitchen. "We have enough."

"I know," Annie took a seat on the closest chair. "But I wanted to cook that meal for Mary and her family. I should have been more prepared."

Andrew furrowed his eyebrows before looking down. "It's all my fault."

"What? No, none of it is your fault."

"You were prepared to cook the meal," Andrew smiled sadly. "But you weren't prepared for me to get shot. I ruined everything."

Annie shook her head slowly. "That is silly."

The couple sat in silence as the sound of the clock on the wall became the loudest thing in the room.

"I've never had a big Christmas," Annie said quietly. "It may sound silly... but this is the first Christmas I can remember looking forward to."

Andrew placed his arm on the table and grabbed Annie's hand. She took it with a smile. "Why is that?"

"I don't know," Annie sighed. "I just figured that there would be a lot of us... a big family. That's all I ever wanted."

"What about your own family? Are you the only child?"

Annie nodded slowly as she shifted her gaze to the window. She could see snow falling down outside. "It has just been my father and me for a while. We never really celebrated. There was no point to it. Life was empty."

"I felt the same way," Andrew gave her a sad smile. "Even though Mary lived nearby, I was always alone for most of the holidays."

Annie looked back at him. For some reason, she had never considered that Andrew would have felt the same as she did during Christmas. Now, it made sense.

He spent most of his time at the office as the town's sheriff. Plus, he didn't have a wife.

Christmas must have been lonely for a long time.

"At least we have each other now," Annie grinned. "That's all that matters. I don't need a big meal to have the perfect Christmas."

Andrew squeezed her hand once. They smiled at each other. A few seconds later, there was a loud knock at the door.

Both of them jumped up in their seats. They weren't expecting visitors.

"Who is that?" Andrew leaned forward in his seat, preparing himself to stand up.

Annie placed a hand on his chest and pushed him back gently. "Stay here. I'll go check."

Before Andrew could complain, Annie rushed over to the front door. She grabbed the handle and pulled it towards herself. The pack of people on her doorstep took her by surprise. For a second, she thought that she was dreaming.

"Good evening!" Mary smiled widely, hugging one of her children to her hip. "I hope you don't mind this... we wanted to drop off a few items."

Annie held onto the doorframe as she looked at all the people. She knew them all. The town's stagecoach driver, Michael, stood behind Mary with a big plate of corn in his hands. Deputy John was standing next to him with a plate of turkey. A few other locals were bouncing up and down on their feet to keep themselves warm.

All of them were carrying something.

"I don't understand," Annie glanced between them, a small smile forming on her face. "What is this?"

Mary looked down at the pie that she was holding with one hand. "I knew that you and Andrew didn't have much time to prepare for Christmas. So... we thought that we'd bring you some food so that you didn't have to cook."

Annie was speechless. Her eyes moved over to look at Michael, who was grinning from ear to ear.

"Got the best corn here, ma'am," he said. "There should be enough here for everyone."

"Everyone?" Annie laughed softly. "There's only two of us here."

Mary giggled at Annie's reaction. "Well, not exactly... you see, I figured that we'd spend this Christmas together. If you're up for inviting some guests, of course."

Annie blinked as she looked around at all of the food. She felt so welcome in the small town. It was very heartwarming. Annie had not lived here for long, and yet, her neighbors were so keen to help her out this Christmas.

It was like one big family. It was just how she dreamed it.

She heard Andrew walking behind her to look over her shoulder. Quickly, she turned around to press her shoulder beneath his arm to support him.

"What's going on, Mary?" he asked, looking around at all of the locals.

Annie could tell that he was smiling too.

"We're here to celebrate," she replied. "Do you have enough chairs?"

Andrew nodded with a grin.

"There you go," Mary grinned. "There will be enough seats for everybody."

"I don't know what to say," Andrew replied. Annie had never heard his voice so quiet before. He was truly taken aback. "This is very generous of you all."

"That's what Christmas is all about, is it not?" Mary asked.

Annie giggled softly as she nodded.

Even though her husband was barely standing, and she never got enough time to cook her own food, none of it mattered in the end.

The kindness from the locals was more than enough to make it feel like Christmas.

Epilogue

One Year Later...

The warmth of the fireplace pulled Annie into a hug as she stirred the vegetables in the water. It was Christmas again, and she had a feeling that it was going to be far better than any other Christmases from the past. Last year, that seemed impossible. However, a lot had changed for the better since last year.

Annie smiled widely when she looked down at her baby boy. He was sleeping peacefully in her arms. He was just like his father. Not even the loudest bang would have been enough to wake him up.

"Is this the letter that you wanted to send?" Andrew asked as he walked into the kitchen.

Annie looked over at him to see that he was holding an envelope in one hand. It was a letter for her father.

She nodded quickly. "Yes, I suppose that I should post it tomorrow. Is the money inside?"

"It is," Andrew replied before placing it on one of the counters. "Do you think that will be enough?"

"It should last him for a while," she smiled. "He's not gambling anymore, after all."

Annie stepped away from the vegetables and sighed. She had not seen her father in a while, but she couldn't help thinking it was for the best. She wanted him to get better with his drinking. Day by day, he was healing. It all became evident when he began to ask for less money.

He didn't need it anymore. He was cutting down on his bad habits. It put a smile on Annie's face.

"Mary should be here soon," Andrew said before coming closer and wrapping his arm around his wife.

They both looked down at their son as they stood in the middle of the kitchen. It was the calm before the storm. Soon enough, the whole house would be filled with laughter and chatter.

"Everything is ready," Annie replied. "I just need to drain the vegetables, and then I'll be done."

Andrew grinned before leaning down to plant a kiss on the side of her head. "You've done an incredible job. I can't wait to try it all."

Annie giggled. "You've tried it all already. I've seen you sneaking into the kitchen to dip your finger into the mashed potatoes!"

"No, that doesn't count," Andrew replied. "I need to taste it with everything else on top. Otherwise, I won't get all of the flavors."

"Oh, alright, I see," Annie giggled. "I didn't realize that you were a professional food taster."

"That I am, ma'am," he said. "That I am."

All of a sudden, there was a knock on the front door. Annie could hear Mary's children laughing behind it from where she stood. It brought a big smile to her face.

Quickly, she looked down at her own son. She wasn't surprised to see that the knock hadn't stirred him from his sleep.

"I'll open it," Andrew said before walking over to the door. "Get ready for the madness."

"I'm always ready," Annie replied. "Let them in."

She didn't have to look in his direction to know that Mary's two children had jumped up to hug Andrew's legs as soon as the door opened. Annie loved the bond that he shared with his cousin's family. It was unbreakable. Now, Annie was a part of it too.

"It smells so delicious in here!" Mary exclaimed as she stepped into the room. When she met Annie's eyes, her hands went up into the air. "Happy Christmas!"

Annie couldn't help but giggle. "Happy Christmas to you too."

She hugged her son closer to her chest as all the guests gathered around her to look at the baby. Mary covered her mouth with both hands as she gushed over him. Her husband stood behind her, his hands on her shoulders.

At that moment, the baby opened his eyes.

"Hi, little Arthur," Mary sang. "You are so cute... I could look at you all day long!"

Annie felt the same. Ever since his arrival, she had been awestruck by his beauty. She had fallen in love for the second time.

"Such a beautiful family," Mary said, tilting her head to the side.

Annie looked up to see that Andrew was standing across the room. He had one of Mary's children in his arms, and he was looking directly at his wife.

Annie knew exactly what he was thinking because the same thoughts were in her head.

This was going to be the best Christmas ever. Again.

The End

FREE GIFT

Just to say thanks for checking our works we like to gift you

Our Exclusive Never Before Released Books

100% FREE!

Please GO TO

http://cleanromancepublishing.com/gift

And get your FREE gift

Thanks for being such a wonderful client.

Please Check out My Other Works

By checking out the link below

http://cleanromancepublishing.com/fjauth

Thank You

Many thanks for taking the time to buy and read through this book.

It means lots to be supported by SPECIAL readers like YOU.

Hope you enjoyed the book; please support my writing by leaving an honest review to assist other readers.

.

With Regards,
Faith Johnson